KV-192-912

GRUMBLERUG'S GANG
and the Great-Hairy-Thing

Karen Wallace
Illustrated by Kim Blundell

CollinsChildren'sBooks
An imprint of HarperCollinsPublishers

For Anna Hextall

First published in Great Britain by CollinsChildren'sBooks 1996

3 5 7 9 8 6 4 2

CollinsChildren'sBooks is a division of
HarperCollins*Publishers* Ltd, 77-85 Fulham Palace Road,
Hammersmith, London W6 8JB

Text copyright © Karen Wallace 1996
Illustrations copyright © Kim Blundell 1996

The author and illustrator assert the moral right to be
identified as the author and illustrator of the work.

Printed and bound in Great Britain
by Caledonian International Book Manufacturing Ltd,
Glasgow G64

ISBN Hardback   0 00 185632 4
        Paperback   0 00 675140 7

Chapter One

It was the beginning of a long hot summer's day. Chips and Rocky Blockhead and their friends Billy, Tilly and Little Millie Ribcage lay on top of a huge bear-rug called Grumblerug.

"I'm fed up," said Chips, scraping a piece of wood with his bone knife.

"It's not fair," muttered Billy, pulling the crust off his leaf sandwich.

"I'm hungry," complained Rocky as he dropped a handful of pebbles on Grumblerug's back.

"He didn't even say thank you," added Tilly. "He never says thank you."

Little Millie leant over and tickled Grumblerug's ear. "Let's ask Grumblerug. He'll know what to do."

"Humph," grumbled Grumblerug. "You could stop dropping wood flakes, sandwich crusts and pebbles all over my back for a start."

"That won't help," moaned Chips.

"It will help *me*," said Grumblerug. "Then perhaps I might be able to help *you*."

Quickly, Chips cleaned up his wood flakes.

Billy picked up his sandwich crusts.

Rocky brushed away the pebbles he had scattered.

"Well?" said Billy.

"Humph," muttered Grumblerug. "Well, sit still and tell me what the problem is."

"A great-hairy-thing is stealing our mammoth burgers," cried Tilly.

"Straight off the cooking fire," said Chips. "The mums and dads are getting very cross and we're getting very hungry."

"Why don't you chase after him?" suggested Grumblerug.

"The great-hairy-thing is *huge*," cried Billy. "Once he tried to catch us but we ran away."

"Anyway, we can't catch him. He drives a chariot with twin mammoths," explained Tilly.

"What's a chariot?" asked Little Millie.

"A big cart with wheels," said Chips.

"Humph," said Grumblerug.

"Why don't you ask the mums and dads—?"

"That's a brilliant idea!" shouted Rocky. "We'll ask the mums and dads to build us a chariot!"

Before Grumblerug had time to finish his sentence, the children had run off. Once again, he was covered in wood flakes, crusts and pebbles.

Chapter Two

The next day, Grumblerug heard a bumping and scraping sound. The dads had made a chariot all by themselves. The mums were too busy picking berries.

The chariot *looked* brilliant but it didn't *sound* brilliant.

"Something's wrong with the dads' chariot," said Rocky.

"The wheels don't go round," said Tilly. "We'll never be able to catch the great-hairy-thing now."

"We could always try throwing rocks at him," said Chips.

"Or big heavy sticks," said Billy.

"We might hurt him like that,"
said Little Millie. "Maybe he's just
hungry."

"He can't be hungry if he's eating
our mammoth burgers," said Rocky.

"Humph," muttered
Grumblerug. "Before I was so
rudely interrupted this morning, I
was going to suggest—"

"What?" the children shouted
together.

Grumblerug rolled his eyes. "I was going to suggest," he repeated slowly, "that you ask the mums and dads if you can go and *talk* to the great-hairy-thing. He might tell you *why* he takes the mammoth burgers. He might even tell you how to make wheels that go round."

This was something no-one had thought of.

"There's only one problem," said Chips. "We don't know where he lives."

"That's not a problem," said Grumblerug. "My friend Tornit the Vulture told me that the great-hairy-thing lives in a cave on Tiger-Tooth Mountain."

"How will we know which cave?" asked Tilly, who liked to get things straight.

"You'll know," said Grumblerug. "The great-hairy-thing has a *very* loud voice."

So Chips, Rocky, Billy, Tilly and Little Millie set off to find the great-hairy-thing.

Two hours later they were standing at the foot of the mountain.

"ARRGH! ARRGH!" A terrible roar boomed above their ears.

"I think we've come to the right place," said Chips, slowly.

"So do I," said Tilly, her face going as white as a cloud.

"ARRGH! ARRGH!" A boulder rolled and bounced down the mountain.

"Stop that roaring!" shouted Little Millie in her loudest voice. "You'll only get a sore throat." It was just the sort of thing the mums always said.

Little Millie wondered whether the great-hairy-thing had a mum to teach him how to behave.

A loud *sniff* came from inside the cave. "What do you want?" shouted a sulky voice.

"We want to talk to you," said Rocky.

"You'd better come up then," said the voice.

The children climbed up the mountain path, over the ledge, and walked right inside the cave.

Chapter Three

It was dark and damp inside the cave. There was no fire but there was a faint smell of mammoth burgers.

Little Millie peered into the gloom. She could just see an enormous figure sitting on a rock. Its huge head was resting in its huge hands. It was sniffing and it was very, very hairy.

The great-hairy-thing did not
look happy.

"Why are you stealing our
mammoth burgers?" asked Chips,
sternly. "You're bigger than us. You
ought to know better."

"You're *mean* to me," said the
great-hairy-thing. "Besides, there
are five of you, and only one of
me."

"Why are we mean?" said Tilly.
"I'm cold up here and you won't
teach me your fire secret," moaned
the great-hairy-thing.

"You never asked us," said Chips.
"I tried to," cried the great-hairy-
thing. "But you all ran away."
"We were frightened of you," said
Little Millie, quietly.

The great-hairy-thing jumped up.
"What do you mean *frightened*?" he
asked.

The children looked at each other. For
a moment no-one knew what to say.
Finally Chips said, "What do you
do when you see a sabre-toothed
tiger?"

The great-hairy-thing leapt onto a rock. He threw a big stick at the ground and wrapped his arms round his body.

"Exactly," said Chips. "*That's* what 'frightened' means."

"Oh," said the great-hairy-thing. "I didn't mean to frighten you. I just wanted your fire secret. Then when you ran away, I was so cross I took your mammoth burgers instead." He stared at his huge feet. "After that, it became a sort of a habit, I suppose."

"Not a very nice habit," said Little Millie sternly. It was just the sort of thing the mums would have said. "The mums and dads were very angry and we were very hungry."

Chips thought hard. "Why don't you meet our mums and dads? " he said. "I'm sure they'd forgive you. Especially if you taught them *your* secret."

"What secret?" asked the great-hairy-thing.

"Your wheel secret."

"If you come back with us now," suggested Billy, "we can trade secrets and sort everything out."

The great-hairy-thing grunted, but he didn't move.

Little Millie felt sorry for him. "What's wrong?" she asked.

"I'm too hairy," sniffed the great-hairy-thing. "I look silly, I know I do."

"You could have a haircut," suggested Rocky.

The great-hairy-thing looked up. "What's a haircut?" he asked.

Chapter Four

Little Millie held Chips' bone knife
in her hand and stepped back to
admire her work.

    She was standing ankle-deep in
hair. "What do you think?" she
asked the others.

    "A little more off the back and
shoulders," suggested Tilly.

"A bit more off the knees," added Chips.

The great-hairy-thing was as good as gold. He didn't complain once how long it was all taking.

At last Little Millie finished. She handed back Chips' knife. "One thing is certain," she said.

"What's that?" asked the great-hairy-thing in a trembling voice.

"You will have to change your name," said Little Millie. "We can't call you great-hairy-thing anymore."

There were no mirrors in the cave so the great-hairy-thing couldn't see his haircut. He could only *feel* it. He ran his huge hands over his new short hair.

"Oh dear," he said. "I'm not very good at names. How about hardly-hairy-thing?"

The children shook their heads. "Hardly-hairy-thing isn't a proper name," said Billy. But he couldn't think of a good name either.

Everyone stared at the floor and thought hard.

"I know!" cried Little Millie, clapping her hands. "What about Harry? It sounds a bit like hairy, and it's a proper name."

"H-a-r-r-y," said the great-hairy-thing, rolling the name in his mouth like a sweet with a strange flavour. "H-a-r-r-y," he said again. This time he smacked his lips.

"Well?" asked Rocky. "Do you like it?"

The great-hairy-thing jumped up. There was a big grin on his face. "I love it!" he cried. "Let's go! My chariot is waiting!"

Chapter Five

Harry led the children out of his cave and down the side of the mountain.

In the middle of a field was a chariot made out of driftwood and bone. The seats were padded with green moss.

The twin mammoths looked suprised to see them. They had just eaten a huge meal of grass and flowers, but they were quite happy to pull the chariot back to the children's cave.

None of the children had ever been in a chariot before. Little Millie was a tiny bit frightened. As she climbed up the steps she pretended she was climbing a tree.

As they thundered across the grass, she closed her eyes and pretended she was rolling down a sand dune. After that everything was fine.

Chips and Billy watched as trees and rocks flashed by. They remembered how long it had taken them to walk to the great-hairy-thing's cave.

They thought of all the heavy loads of wood they had to carry for the dads.

They thought of how they had to drag their books to school every day. Wheels that went round would change everything.

"Are you thinking what I'm thinking?" shouted Rocky over the roar of the bumpy chariot.

A big smile spread across the faces of all the children.

"You bet," Billy said. "The dads would love a chariot that went as fast as this."

"So would the mums," cried Tilly. "They could have a bones'n'berries cart!"

"And a get-there-faster thing for everybody!" cried Little Millie.

The twin mammoths started to slow down. They had almost arrived at the children's cave.

"Oh no!" cried Harry, pointing to a ledge above the cave. "What are we going to do now?"

The children looked up. The mums and dads were waving sticks in the air and shouting.

"Oh dear," whispered Little Millie. "They *are* a bit cross, aren't they?"

Chapter Six

At that moment, a huge vulture flapped out of a tree and landed on top of one of the mammoths.

"I'm Tornit," he squawked. "Who are you? This chariot belongs to the great-hairy-thing in the cave."

"No it doesn't," said Little Millie. "It belongs to Harry now. Harry has come to say 'sorry' to the mums and dads for stealing our mammoth burgers."

Tornit looked over at the mums and dads. They were still shouting and waving sticks. Then he looked at Harry. He cocked his head to one side.

"It seems to me that Harry needs help," he squawked. "What do you think?"

Everyone started shouting at once.
"Hold it, hold it," said Tornit,
lifting a wing for silence.

"Why don't I just fly over to that ledge and tell the mums and dads what's going on? Then you can shout at *them*, and not at *me*." Without another word, he flapped into the air.

A moment later one by one the mums and dads dropped their sticks and climbed down from the ledge.

"Do you really think the mums and dads will forgive me?" whispered Harry to Little Millie. He sounded nervous and kept running his hand through his hair.

"Of course they will," said Little Millie in her firmest voice.

They all jumped down from the chariot and ran over to their cave.

"This is our new friend Harry," said Chips, quickly.

Harry stared at the mums and dads.

The mums and dads stared at
Harry.

"But where is the great-hairy-
thing?" asked Mrs Blockhead.

"This is *his* chariot," added Mrs
Ribcage.

"The great-hairy-thing has gone forever," said Rocky.

"His name is Harry now," said Billy, "and he has something to trade with you."

"Trade?" said Mr Blockhead. He looked suspicious. "What does this Harry have that *we* want?"

"What do we have that *he* wants?" asked Mr Ribcage.

"He has the wheel secret," cried Little Millie, jumping up and down, "and you have the fire secret!"

"And he's *very* sorry he stole all our mammoth burgers," said Tilly quickly.

The mums and dads thought for a moment. Then they all laughed.

"A trade!" cried Mr Blockhead. "What a brilliant idea!"

"Don't worry about the mammoth burgers, dear," said Mrs Ribcage, kindly.

"I'm sure you were just hungry and lonely," added Mrs Blockhead with a smile.

Harry nodded and stared at his
feet so no-one could see his lips
trembling.

"Whoopee!" shouted Little Millie.
"Now we can have a mammoth
burger barbecue to celebrate. I'm
starving!"

Chapter Seven

It was the end of a long summer's day. Chips, Tilly and Little Millie lay stretched out on top of Grumblerug.

Chips was busy making a model chariot out of wood. He didn't notice the pile of shavings that dropped on to Grumblerug.

Tilly was scratching a picture of a bones'n'berries cart on a flat piece of sandy rock. She didn't notice the bits of grit that fell onto Grumblerug.

Little Millie tickled Grumblerug's ears. "Aren't you proud of us, Grumblerug?" she said. "We've changed everything. Now *everybody's* happy."

"Humph," muttered Grumblerug,
feeling the wood shavings and the
grit all over his back. "Nothing
much seems to have changed to me."
Chips looked up from his chariot.

Tilly looked up from her picture.

"You're wrong, Grumblerug," said
Little Millie, tweaking one of his
ears. "Now that we've made friends
with Harry, nothing is going to be
the same again."

"Just you wait and see," added Chips with a laugh.

There was a squeaking and creaking noise from round the corner.

Billy and Rocky were pushing something low and flat that bumped over the ground on four as-round-as-they-could-get-them wheels.

Every hair on Grumblerug's back stood up and shook. "What's that?" he asked slowly.

"It's a bear-rug buggy," said Billy proudly. "Harry helped us make it."

"What's a bear-rug buggy?" growled Grumblerug.

"It's a buggy for carting rugs round," said Rocky. "Especially bear-rugs."

Grumblerug could feel the hairs on his back popping out of their roots. He did not want to move. He did not want to be carted round.

How was he going to talk the
children out of it?

There was a thunder of mammoth
hooves. A chariot screeched to a
halt in a cloud of dust. Harry
jumped down in front of them.

"Look at my new inventions," he
cried, waving his arms.

The children looked.

Strapped on to the back of the chariot were five of the strangest looking things they had ever seen. Instead of two wheels beside each other, they had two wheels in front of each other. They looked *really* exciting.

Harry lifted his inventions down.

A minute later, Chips, Rocky,
Billy, Tilly and Little Millie were
sitting on them.

"Now what do we do?" asked
Tilly.

"Push the pedals with your feet,"
said Harry. "Steer with the
handlebars and ride over to my cave
tomorrow." He threw back his head
and laughed. "I'm having my first
ever bonfire party!"

"What about Grumblerug?"
shouted Rocky. "Can he come too?
We've built him a bear-rug buggy."
Grumblerug winked at Harry
and shook his head once, from side
to side.

"Absolutely not!" cried Harry, winking back. "A flea-bitten old rug like him wouldn't like it. He might get burned by mistake!"

For the rest of the day, Grumblerug watched the children riding Harry's new inventions. He had never seen them so happy.

Little Millie was right. Things were never going to be the same again.

"Humph!" muttered Grumblerug to himself. "I *suppose* that's all right."